MARY ENGELBREIT'S
NURSERY TALES

MARY ENGELBREIT'S
NURSERY TALES

A TREASURY OF CHILDREN'S CLASSICS

With an introduction by
LEONARD S. MARCUS

HarperCollinsPublishers

I'd like to thank everyone at Mary Engelbreit Studios, with a special thank-you to Pam Dobek and Jackie Ahlstrom. I'd also like to thank my amazing editor at HarperCollins, Barbara Lalicki, who always turns out to be right in the end!

Mary Engelbreit's Nursery Tales
Copyright © 2008 by Mary Engelbreit Ink

Introduction copyright © 2008 by Leonard S. Marcus
Leonard S. Marcus is one of the children's book world's most respected historians and critics.
His books include *Margaret Wise Brown: Awakened by the Moon*; *Dear Genius: The Letters of Ursula Nordstrom*; *Ways of Telling*; and *Storied City*.

Manufactured in China.
For information address HarperCollins Children's Books, a division of HarperCollins Publishers,
10 East 53rd Street, New York, NY 10022.
www.harpercollinschildrens.com

Library of Congress Cataloging-in-Publication Data is available.
ISBN 978-0-06-073168-7 (trade) — ISBN 978-0-06-073169-4 (lib. bdg.)

Design by Stephanie Bart-Horvath
10 11 12 13 SCP 10 9 8 7 6 5 4
❖
First Edition

for TESS and JACK
~with love~

TABLE of

CONTENTS

INTRODUCTION

Childhood has its treasures. Here are a perfect dozen of them for you to share with your child—classic tales of once upon a time for reading aloud, poring over, pondering, and remembering.

Chances are you already know some of the characters: Little Red Riding Hood, Hansel and Gretel, the Little Red Hen, and the Three Bears, into whose forest cottage young Goldilocks wanders for an innocent look around. I can recall reveling, as a four-year-old, in the hilarious confrontation that ensues when that lumbering bear family returns home to find their once-tidy house, with its matched sets of three of everything, reduced to chaos by a visitor not much older, or wilder, than I.

Stories like these take children out of their everyday concerns about buttons that won't button and itches that mustn't be scratched, and transport them to another, more dreamlike

realm where the imaginable is possible. One of the chief fascinations of these old tales lies in the breathtaking ease with which they blend reality and unreality. Talking animals? The better to tell us what real mischief the world's wolves may have in store. Magic beanstalk? The better to let us see our planet for what it is: a vast and mysterious place, yet one (the stories assure us) that is neither *too* vast nor *too* mysterious, provided we just keep our wits about us.

In the most vivid way possible, these tales about Jack, the Little Red Hen, the Three Little Pigs, and company dramatize (without seeming to teach) the true meaning of bravery, loyalty, generosity, hope, friendship, determination, recklessness, greed, deceit, and just plain foolishness. What child hasn't felt like the hero of "The Ugly Duckling," a lonely outsider in an uncaring world? What preschooler won't immediately see through the vanity of the preening emperor who cannot himself see that he's naked; or experience a touch of scorn for the two careless piglets who lack the sense to build themselves strong houses; or feel a surge of admiration for Hansel and Gretel's skill at charting a way out of a scary situation?

How scary, you ask? Generations of parents have posed this question with regard to traditional tales involving witches, ogres, wolves, and the like. Asking it now brings us round

to the pivotal role that illustration can play in setting the stage and tone for a collection like this one. From first to last, Mary Engelbreit is an artist of kindliness and comfort. The landscapes glimpsed in her meticulously rendered pictures more closely resemble a park or playground than a wild wood. *Really* scary things couldn't possibly happen there.

Engelbreit knows a cozy home when she sees one. In the world she has imagined for these stories, everything is in its place: the sporty, well-coordinated outfits her characters wear, the well-tended gardens they raise, and the piping hot food they put on their tables. Her child-friendly interiors come well furnished with comfy chairs, snug beds, and bric-a-brac aplenty, the accumulated stuff of years of living, which for the children of the house so often become cherished springboards to fantasy.

Let the big bad wolf huff and puff if he must. Happy endings await.

—Leonard S. Marcus

Author, critic, and children's literature historian

Welcome!
Some stories are like dear friends — always familiar and always as much fun as they were on the first day you met them. Here are 12 of my best friends. I hope they'll become your favorites, too!

Mary Engelbreit

1

GOLDILOCKS and the THREE BEARS

Once upon a time there were three bears: a great big Papa Bear, a medium-size Mama Bear, and a tiny, wee Baby Bear. One morning the three bears left their porridge to cool and went out walking.

While they were out, a little girl called Goldilocks
came upon the empty house. "I wonder who lives
here," she said. She walked around to the back door
and, forgetting her manners, let herself into the kitchen.
On the table Goldilocks saw three bowls of porridge.

First she tasted the porridge in the great big bowl. But it was too hot.

Then she tried the porridge in the medium-size bowl. But it was too cold.

Then she tasted the porridge in the tiny, wee bowl. "This is just right!" said Goldilocks. And she ate it all up.

Then Goldilocks saw three chairs. First she sat in the great big chair. But it was too hard. Then she tried the medium-size chair. But it was too soft. Then she sat in the tiny, wee chair. "This is just right!" said Goldilocks. But no sooner did she say those words, than—*craaaack!* The tiny, wee chair broke into bits!

All this excitement made Goldilocks sleepy, so she climbed the stairs to the bedroom. There she saw three beds.

First she lay down on the great big bed. But it was too hard.

Then she tried the medium-size bed. But it was too soft.

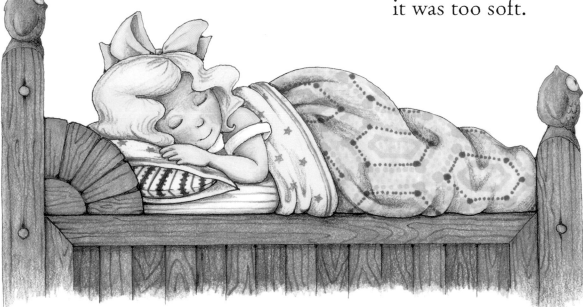

Then she lay down on the tiny, wee bed. "This is just right!" said Goldilocks, and she soon fell fast asleep.

After a while, the three bears came back. When Papa Bear saw his bowl, he roared, "SOMEBODY'S BEEN EATING MY PORRIDGE!" And Mama Bear growled, "Somebody's been eating *my* porridge!" And Baby Bear squeaked, "Somebody's been eating *my* porridge and ate it all up!"

When Papa Bear saw his chair, he roared, "SOMEBODY'S BEEN SITTING IN MY CHAIR!"

And Mama Bear growled, "Somebody's been sitting in *my* chair!"

And Baby Bear—well, you know what happened to *his* chair. He squeaked, "Somebody's been sitting in *my* chair and broke it all to bits!"

So they all went into the bedroom, and when Papa
Bear saw his bed he roared, "SOMEBODY'S BEEN
SLEEPING IN MY BED!" And Mama Bear
growled, "Somebody's been sleeping in *my* bed!"
And Baby Bear squeaked, "Somebody's been sleep-
ing in *my* bed—and there she is!"

Goldilocks heard the noise and
woke with a start. When she saw the
three bears, she sprang from the bed,
jumped out the window, and ran home as
fast as her legs would carry her.

Her mother and father were happy
to see her. And the three bears
lived happily ever after, too.

the THREE LITTLE PIGS

THERE ONCE were three little pigs who lived with their mother in a tiny house. As the little pigs grew bigger, the house grew smaller, and soon it came time for them to go out into the world and build houses of their own.

The first little pig hastily built her house of straw. The second little pig took a bit more time. He built a house of sticks. And the third little pig, who was smarter than the others, took the longest. She built a house of bricks.

Now, the first little pig was just sitting down to breakfast in her new straw house when she heard the voice of the Big Bad Wolf outside.

"Little pig, little pig, may I come in?" called the Big Bad Wolf.

"Not by the hair on my chinny-chin-chin!" cried the first little pig.

"Then I'll huff and I'll puff and I'll blow your house down," growled the Big Bad Wolf. And that's just what he did.

"Oh, help! Help!" squealed the first little pig, and do you know what? She ran to the house of sticks, where her brother took her in.

A little while later the brother and sister were just sitting down to lunch in the new stick house when they heard the Big Bad Wolf outside.

"Little pig, little pig, may I come in?" called the Big Bad Wolf.

"Not by the hair on my chinny-chin-chin!" cried the second little pig.

"Then I'll huff and I'll puff and I'll blow your house down," growled the Big Bad Wolf. And that's just what he did.

"Oh, help!" squealed the little pigs. And they ran and ran to the brick house, where their sister took them in.

A little while later the three little pigs were just

YOUR HOUSE DOWN!

sitting down to a bubbling-hot stew. Sure enough, they heard the Big Bad Wolf outside.

"Little pig, little pig, may I come in?" called the Big Bad Wolf.

"No, you may not," said the third little pig. "Not by the hair on my chinny-chin-chin."

"Then I'll huff and I'll puff and I'll blow your house down," growled the Big Bad Wolf.

"Go ahead and try," said the third little pig calmly.

The wolf huffed and he puffed, but try as he might, he could not blow that little brick house down.

Then the three little pigs heard noises on the roof, for the wolf had thought to try the chimney. Down tumbled the wolf, right into the cooking pot. He hopped out and scurried away, and that was the end of the Big Bad Wolf.

The three little pigs sang and played their favorite songs long into the night.

3

PUSS in BOOTS

THERE ONCE WAS a young man who had nothing in the world but a cat named Puss. He felt very sorry for himself. He sighed. "What good is a cat?"

Hearing this, Puss replied, "A cat is a very fine thing indeed.

"Give me a pair of boots and a sack, and I will make your fortune." As soon as Puss got his boots, he set off.

First he caught a fine rabbit and put it in the sack. Then he boldly made his way to the castle. "I have come to see the King!" he cried. "I bring a gift from my master, the Marquis of Carabas!"

The King was pleased with the gift and invited
Puss in Boots to stay for supper. The cat ate his fill
from the banquet table, and while he ate, he talked.

First he told the King how rich the Marquis of
Carabas was.

Then he told the
Queen how noble
the Marquis of
Carabas was.

Then he told the Princess his master
was handsome, brave, and charming.
By the time Puss in Boots left the
castle, everyone was talking about the
mysterious Marquis.

Puss had learned that the royal family was about to take a tour of the countryside. He ran back to his master and said, "I have a plan. Go swimming in the river today, and I will make your wildest dreams come true."

While the young man swam, Puss hid his clothes. Then Puss jumped in front of the King's carriage and shouted, "Help! The Marquis of Carabas is drowning!"

Quick as a flash, the King's footman jumped in the river and pulled the young man out. "Someone has stolen my clothes!" the young man cried.

So the King gave the young man new clothes to wear and let him sit in his own royal carriage. In his borrowed clothes, the Marquis of Carabas looked just as rich and noble and handsome as Puss had promised.

Meanwhile, the cat ran on ahead down the road, until he came to some fields that were owned by a fearsome ogre, the terror of the land. He told all the farmers about his plan, and they agreed to help him.

Next Puss in Boots ran ahead to the Ogre's castle. He knocked boldly on the door and the Ogre answered.

"Is it true that you can turn into anything you like?" Puss asked.

The Ogre proudly turned into a lion.

"But it must be easy for an Ogre to turn into a lion," said Puss in Boots. "An Ogre could never turn into something tiny, like a mouse."

The lion roared and turned into a mouse. In a flash, Puss ate him up, and that was the end of the Ogre.

Along the road, the King saw farmers working. When he asked who owned the land, the farmers did just as Puss had told them and said, "The Marquis of Carabas!"

Puss in Boots stood by the Ogre's castle gate. When the King came by, Puss called, "The Marquis of Carabas welcomes you!"

The King and the Queen and the Princess ate a marvelous supper in the castle with the Marquis and his cat. Before long the Princess and the Marquis of Carabas were engaged to be married.

On the day of his wedding, the Marquis of Carabas turned to Puss in Boots and said, "Thank you, my friend. You were right—a cat is a very fine thing, indeed!"

—4—
LITTLE RED RIDING HOOD

THERE ONCE was a little girl who always wore a red cloak with a hood, so everyone called her Little Red Riding Hood. One day her mother gave her a basket of biscuits to take to her granny, who was not feeling well.

Little Red Riding Hood set off, and she had not
gone very far before she met a wolf.

"Good morning," said the Wolf. "Where are you
going in such a beautiful red cloak?"

"I'm taking this basket of biscuits to my granny,
who is ill in bed," Little Red Riding Hood replied.

She knew she shouldn't
talk to strangers, but this
one seemed perfectly friendly.

"I hope your granny doesn't
live too far away," said the Wolf.

"Oh no," said Little Red Riding Hood. "She lives
in the cottage at the end of the path."

Now, the Wolf figured a weak old granny
would make an easy meal. So away he ran, taking
a shortcut straight to Granny's cottage. He
knocked at her door.

"Who's there?" Granny called.

"It's your little granddaughter,"
said the Wolf in a high voice.

"Lift the latch and let yourself in, dear," said Granny.

The Wolf lifted the latch, found Granny inside, and swallowed her in one gulp. Then he put on Granny's nightcap and climbed into her bed. Before long, Little Red Riding Hood knocked at the door.

"Lift the latch and let yourself in," called the Wolf.

Little Red Riding Hood lifted the latch and walked into the cottage. She took a few steps toward the bed and said, "Why, Granny, what big eyes you have."

"All the better to see you with, my dear," said the Wolf.

"And Granny, what big ears you have."

"All the better to hear you with, my dear."

"And Granny, what big teeth you have."

ALL THE BETTER TO EAT YOU WITH, MY DEAR!

"All the better to eat you with,
my dear!" growled the Wolf.
He jumped out of bed and ate Little Red
Riding Hood in one big gulp.

That might have been the end of Little Red Riding Hood, but luckily a woodcutter chopping wood near the cottage heard the Wolf's growls and came to look. When he saw the Wolf in Granny's glasses, he gave him a big scolding, and the Wolf let Little Red Riding Hood and her granny step out unharmed. Embarrassed, the Wolf ran away.

Do you remember the biscuits? They were still in the basket waiting—and they made a fine treat.

the EMPEROR'S NEW CLOTHES

Once there was an Emperor who wanted the best of everything—the tallest castle, the biggest army, the funniest jester, and especially the finest clothes. Knowing this, a clever tailor decided to play a trick on him.

The tailor came to the palace with his prettiest silks and satins. "Don't you have something better?" asked the Emperor. "Something nobody else has?"

"In this bag," the tailor said, "I have the finest cloth in the world. It is as thin as moonbeams and as light as air."

"Show me!" the Emperor demanded.

The tailor pretended to pull the cloth out of his bag. "Look at the colors!" he said. "Look at the pattern! Isn't it the loveliest thing you've ever seen?

"Anyone who wears it will feel as if he is wearing nothing at all. And there is one more thing." The tailor whispered in the Emperor's ear, "Only the wise can see this cloth. It is invisible to fools."

The Emperor could see nothing. But if I tell the tailor that, he thought, he'll think I am a fool! He'll know I'm not wise enough to be the Emperor! So the Emperor said, "Make me a suit of this cloth at once!"

The next day the tailor sent a box to the palace. Inside it, he said, was a suit made of the magical cloth. The Emperor pretended to put the suit on. His wife could not see a thing. No one could. But they all wanted the others to think they were wise enough to see the cloth, so they cried out, "Wonderful! Our Emperor has the most beautiful clothes in the world!"

The Emperor decided to go on a walk to show off. Now, all the townspeople had heard of the Emperor's new clothes. They did not want to look like fools, so they clapped and cheered as if they could see what the Emperor was wearing.

One little girl came onto her balcony. She could
see that the Emperor had nothing on. And she didn't
care if people thought she was foolish, so she said
loudly, "But he doesn't have any clothes on. The
Emperor has no clothes!"

People in the crowd heard. And they all realized
that *nobody* could see the Emperor's new clothes!

"The Emperor has no clothes!" they shouted.

The Emperor's soldiers heard. His servants heard. His wife heard.

"The Emperor has no clothes!" they gasped.

And the Emperor heard. Then he knew how the tailor had tricked him. He rushed home. For many weeks he hardly dared to show his face. And to this day people tell the story of a foolish Emperor who took a walk one day wearing no clothes at all!

6

HANSEL and GRETEL

There once lived a brother and sister called Hansel and Gretel. Their family was poor, and they only had stale bread to eat. One day Mother sent them out into the woods to pick wild strawberries for supper.

"The woods get dark quickly," Mother said. "Be sure you don't get lost."

Now Hansel was a clever boy, and Gretel was a clever girl. As they walked farther and farther into the woods, they dropped a trail of bread crumbs to follow back to their cottage.

Working together, Hansel and Gretel filled their basket with ripe red berries. By late afternoon they were ready to go home.

"Mother will be happy," Hansel said.

"But where are the bread crumbs?" Gretel cried.

The birds had eaten every crumb. There was no trail to lead the children home.

Lost and afraid, poor Hansel and Gretel at last ate the
berries. Trying to stay cheerful, the children made plans
for the morning, then fell asleep on the forest floor.

When the sun woke them, Hansel and Gretel set off through the woods. They'd wandered all day long when they came to a clearing, and there they saw a wonderful thing. It was a little cottage made of cake and candy! Hansel and Gretel were so hungry that they started breaking off bits of the house to eat.

They heard a strange voice whisper: "Nibble, nibble, like a mouse. Who is nibbling at my house?"

NIBBLE, NIBBLE, Like a Mouse, who is nibbling at my House?

Suddenly the door opened, and out came a very ugly woman who was really a witch. Hansel and Gretel were frightened, but the Witch spoke so sweetly and they were so hungry that they went with her into the house. Inside, the Witch fed them a delicious dinner, with all the foods and sweets they had ever dreamed of.

They were so full that they soon fell asleep. In the morning before they woke, the Witch lit a fire in the oven. "The boy first," she cackled. "He will be tasty!" For it was true—the Witch lured children to her cottage and then gobbled them up!

After the fire was lit, the Witch grabbed the sleeping Hansel and locked him in a cage behind the house. After that she came back and put Gretel to work.

"Get up and set the table!" she screeched. "I'm going to have a feast!"

Now clever Gretel saw Hansel in the cage, and as she set the table, she tried to think what to do.

"See if the oven is hot!" the Witch called to Gretel.

By now Gretel had a plan. So she said, "It is stone cold."

"That can't be," said the Witch, poking her head into the oven.

Quickly Gretel gave her a shove and banged the door shut. Then she set her brother free.

Hansel and Gretel ran away into the forest. Before long they heard their mother calling, searching for them. She was so happy to see her children that she wept with joy.

Then they all walked home together and sat down to eat. Their simple supper tasted so good!

the CITY MOUSE and the COUNTRY MOUSE

ONCE UPON A TIME there was a poor country mouse. Her cousin, the rich city mouse, came to visit.

"Wow!" said the City Mouse, seeing how her cousin lived. "You are really poor!"

"I don't have much to offer," said the Country Mouse. "But I'll go dig up something good to eat."

"Roots!" the City Mouse said when the Country Mouse returned. "At my house we don't have to *dig* for our dinner! Just this morning the Cook baked a cake!"

Now the Country Mouse felt very sorry for herself. "I'd like some cake!" she said.

So the two mice walked back to the city and into the fanciest house the Country Mouse had ever seen.

"This is the life!" said the City Mouse proudly. "And there's the cake!"

"It sure looks tasty," said the Country Mouse.

"We can eat our fill!" said the City Mouse. "As long as the Cook isn't looking," she added.

Just then—*Wham!*—the kitchen door opened and in came the Cook.

"Scat!" she cried, and the two cousins scurried into a hole.

"No problem," whispered the City Mouse. "We'll have another chance in just a second." But when they crept out again, the Cook chased them with a broom.

"Don't worry," said the City Mouse, all out of breath now. "That cake isn't going anywhere."

They waited two hours and got very, very hungry.
Can you guess what happened when they came out
again and started to nibble? In came the Cat!

The cousins ran back into the hole. As they hud-
dled there, hungry and terrified, the Cat sat watching,
ready to pounce.

Country Mouse started thinking fondly of her field and home. At home she could have tasty roots and dry wheat stalks for dinner. So she said to the City Mouse, "Please come visit me often, cousin." As soon as the Cat turned his head, she ran away. Before long, she was safely home, snug and happy.

-8-

JACK and the BEANSTALK

THERE ONCE WAS a noble woman who had fallen on hard times. Her castle had been stolen away by a greedy giant, and now she lived in a cottage with her only son, Jack. He was a lazy boy—always dreaming, never working.

Mother and son grew poorer and poorer until they had nothing but a cow.

Jack's mother told him to sell the cow for a good price, and he agreed. But do you know what?

On the way into town, Jack met a strange little man, who gave him three magic beans in exchange for the cow. Jack thought his mother would be happy to have the beans—after all, they were magic!

"Three beans!" Jack's mother shouted when he got home. "You foolish boy!" Disgusted, she threw the beans out the window.

Now Jack felt sad, and he went straight to bed. But in the morning when he went to the window, he saw that the magic beans had sprung up into a huge vine! There was nothing to do but to climb it.

Higher and higher he climbed, until at last he reached the top of the vine and found himself looking at a castle that was high among the clouds.

Jack didn't know it, but this was the very castle that had been stolen from his mother when he was just a baby.

When Jack got there, he knocked. A giant woman
answered the door. After taking one look at him, she
said, "Please, please, run away! My husband is a cruel
giant!" But Jack was exhausted and hungry, so he
offered to work for food, and she let him in.

FEE FI FI FO FUM!

As he was finishing up his dinner, there came a deafening roar. Jack hid in a cupboard just as the Giant thundered in, bellowing, "Fee—Fi—Fo—Fum, I smell the blood of an Englishman!"

But the Giant's wife said, "It's the stew you smell."

"Hmph!" the Giant grunted, and he sat down to his giant supper. At last he finished eating, and his wife brought out a golden goose.

"Lay!" shouted the Giant. And the goose laid an egg of solid gold! The Giant amused himself for hours, commanding the goose to lay her golden eggs.

Finally the Giant's wife brought out a harp. The Giant said, "Play me a drink!" and a drink appeared. "Play me a pillow!" and a pillow appeared in the Giant's chair. "Play music!" and the harp played lovely music until, at last, the Giant fell asleep.

When the Giant was snoring loudly, Jack crept out of his hiding place, grabbed the golden goose and the harp, and started to run! But the harp twisted in Jack's grasp and started chiming, "Master! Master!"

Jack held tight to the goose and the harp and ran to the beanstalk as fast as he could go.

But the harp's cries woke the Giant. His feet shook the ground as he chased them! The beanstalk trembled with the terrible weight of him! As soon as Jack was safely on the ground, he cut the beanstalk with one swing of his hatchet. The Giant fell to the ground and died instantly!

Jack gave the golden goose to his mother, who instantly recognized it as her own beloved pet. Then he said to the harp, "Play dinner, please." A grand meal appeared before them. The very next day Jack asked the harp to play a gown for his mother, a castle to live in, and happiness to last a lifetime.

the GINGERBREAD BOY

A little old woman and a little old man once lived together in a little old house. One day the old woman made a little gingerbread boy. When she went to take him from the oven, up he jumped and away he ran!

The old woman and the old man ran after him, calling, "Stop, little Gingerbread Boy!"

But the Gingerbread Boy just laughed and sang, "Run, run as fast as you can! You can't catch me, I'm the Gingerbread Man!"

The Gingerbread Boy ran on and on until he met a cow.

"Stop!" said the Cow. "I want to eat you!"

But the little Gingerbread Boy hollered, "Run, run as fast as you can! You can't catch me, I'm the Gingerbread Man!"

Run, run as fast as you can! You can't

The Gingerbread Boy ran on until he met a horse.

"Stop!" said the Horse. "I want to eat you!"

But the little Gingerbread Boy called, "Run, run as fast as you can! You can't catch me, I'm the Gingerbread Man!"

The little Gingerbread Boy ran on until he met a pig.

"Stop!" said the Pig. "I want to eat you!"

But the little Gingerbread Boy shouted, "Run, run as fast as you can! You can't catch me, I'm the Gingerbread Man!"

catch me, I'm the Gingerbread Man!

The little Gingerbread Boy ran on until he met a fox.
"Hello," said the Fox politely.

Well, the little Gingerbread Boy was feeling very bold by now, so he said to the Fox, "I've run away from a little old woman and a little old man and a cow and a horse and a pig, and I can run away from you, I can, I can," and then he started to run, singing his little song, until suddenly he stopped, for he had come to a river.

The Fox caught up to the Gingerbread Boy. "Jump on my tail and I will take you across the water," the Fox said kindly. And the Gingerbread Boy did.

After a minute the Fox said, "The water is deep. Jump on my back." And the Gingerbread Boy did.

Then in the middle of the river the Fox said, "It's getting deeper. Jump on my shoulder!" And the Gingerbread Boy did. Now when they were near the other side, the Fox cried, "The water is even deeper here! Jump on my nose!"

Now, the Gingerbread Boy knew that the minute he jumped onto the clever Fox's nose, the Fox would gobble him up. So he waited until they were almost at the shore. Then he jumped onto the Fox's nose. But before the Fox could eat him, the Gingerbread Boy jumped onto a rock, then onto dry land, and he ran away singing,

"Run, run as fast as you can!
You can't catch me,
I'm the Gingerbread Man!"

−10−
the ELVES and the SHOEMAKER

ONCE UPON A TIME there was a good shoemaker who worked hard but was still poor. All he had in the world was a single piece of leather—just enough to make one more pair of shoes.

He cut out the leather and set it out on his workbench, ready to make into shoes the next day. Then he hugged his wife and went to bed.

The next morning he got up and saw to his surprise that there was a perfectly made pair of shoes on the table! They were so beautiful that a customer bought them right away. Now the Shoemaker could buy leather to make two pairs of shoes.

That evening he cut out the two pairs of shoes and went to bed.

When he got up in the morning, there were the shoes on his work-bench, all finished! And so it went, day after day. Each day the Shoemaker could afford to buy more leather, and each day more shoes apeared. Soon he and his wife were getting rich!

One evening the Shoemaker said to his wife, "Let's stay up and watch tonight. We'll find out who is making the shoes!"

So they hid and watched. Just as the clock struck twelve, two tiny elves danced into the room. The little elves were barely clothed, but they carried their own little scissors and hammers and thread. They hopped up on the bench, picked up the leather, and began to work.

When they were finished, the elves held hands and danced around the shoes.

What a merry sight! The Shoemaker and his wife could barely keep from laughing.

At daybreak the elves danced away out the windows. "How can we ever thank them?" wondered the Shoemaker.

"Here it is cold and almost Christmas, and yet they have no clothes!" said the wife. "I'd like to make them each a tiny coat and a little pair of trousers and socks."

"And I will make tiny shoes," said her husband.

They got right to work. Soon the tiny clothes and shoes were finished. On Christmas Eve the Shoemaker cleaned his bench, and on it he put the two little sets of clothes. Then he and his wife hid and watched. Just at midnight the elves came in.

When they saw the little clothes, they laughed for joy! They put on the clothes and danced around in a circle! Just as the sun came up, they danced out the window and out of sight forever.

From that day on, the good Shoemaker and his wife were, like the elves, always helpful to others and joyful in their hearts. They even took up dancing.

the LITTLE RED HEN

ONCE the Little Red Hen was getting ready to plant some wheat, and she said,

"Cluck-cluck-cluck!

I'll plant this wheat all in a row,

And soon, dear friends, it will start to grow.

Now who will help me sow the wheat?"

"Not I," said the fine, feathered Duck.
"Not I," said the little gray Mouse.
"Not I," said the big pink Pig.

"Then I'll sow it all by myself," said Little Red Hen.
When the wheat had grown, Little Red Hen said,
"Now who will help me cut and thresh the wheat?"

"Not I," said the fine, feathered Duck.
"Not I," said the little gray Mouse.
"Not I," said the big pink Pig.

"Then I'll cut it and thresh it all by myself,"
said Little Red Hen.

When the wheat was cut and threshed, Little Red Hen
said, "Who'll help me carry the grain to the mill?"

"Not I," said the fine, feathered Duck.
"Not I," said the little gray Mouse.
"Not I," said the big pink Pig.

"Then I'll carry it all by myself,"
said Little Red Hen. And so she did.

When the wheat was ground,
Little Red Hen said, "Who will
help me bake the bread?"

"Not I," said the fine, feathered Duck.
"Not I," said the little gray Mouse.
"Not I," said the big pink Pig.

"Then I'll bake it all by myself,"
said Little Red Hen.

When the bread was baked, Little Red
Hen said,

"The bread is done, it's warm and sweet,
Now who will come and help me eat?"

"I will!" said the fine, feathered Duck.
"I will!" said the little gray Mouse.
"I will!" said the big pink Pig.

"Oh no, you won't!" cried Little Red Hen.

"I asked for help time and again,
but no one proved to be my friend.
So I'll eat it all by myself!
Cluck-cluck!"

And so she did.

–12–

the UGLY DUCKLING

ONCE UPON A TIME, five eggs began to hatch. One by one, pretty yellow ducklings came out of their shells. But one egg was not like the others. When it cracked, out came a clumsy little gray bird with a great long neck.

The other animals in the barnyard made fun of the Ugly Duckling. He wished he could belong, but even his own brothers and sisters thought he was an odd duck.

So one day, when everyone was pestering him, the Ugly Duckling decided to run away.

He flew over the hedge and made a little nest for himself, all alone, at the edge of a pond.

Slowly the months passed, and the days grew colder. One evening a flock of strange birds appeared on the pond. They were dazzlingly white, with long, graceful necks.

Never had the Ugly Duckling seen such beauty.

With a strange, sharp cry, the birds spread their wings and flew off. The Ugly Duckling swam madly around on the little pond and then he, too, cried out—a strange, sharp cry. He longed to fly away with the beautiful birds.

All winter long the Ugly Duckling dreamed of those birds. Finally spring came. The little animals and flowers started stirring. One fine day the Ugly Duckling saw two beautiful white birds like those he'd dreamed of all winter.

"Look! The swans have come!" cried some children.

Our duckling was very sad. He felt even uglier and more alone than usual. But as he ducked his head, he saw himself in the water for the very first time that spring. He had a long graceful neck and dazzling white feathers. He was no longer an ugly duckling! He was a swan!

The Ugly Duckling had changed into his grown-up self! He was the same, but different, all at once. "I had no idea I would turn out this way!" said the happy new swan.

Other swans swam over to meet him. They welcomed him to their flock. The children threw bread crumbs to him and cried, "There's a beautiful new swan this year!" He had found where he belonged at last.

A NOTE FROM MARY

When I began working on this book, I wanted to create a collection of tales that would appeal to the child I once was, and to my granddaughter Mikayla's generation, who are so much a part of today's electronic world, and who love spunky characters, adventure, and humor. So I set out to gather stories for children just past the Mother Goose years, choosing favorites I remembered and wanted to illustrate.

I found as I compiled this collection that the stories that I liked as a little girl still made me smile. Back then, I read "The Three Little Pigs" and "Little Red Riding Hood" over and over, so they were my first choices. I love that these twelve stories have a good mix of different kinds of people and animals, and a timeless appeal. They've endured through the years because they are short but still pack a punch. After all this time, they are still perfect for dramatic bedtime storytelling or for reading aloud.

When I set out to illustrate the book, I wanted to make sure to bring out the personality of each character and to use bright colors that would be attractive to kids. I tried to think beyond my immediate memories of a character to see each one more fully. "Goldilocks and the Three Bears" is such a classic, and I could really see Goldilocks in my mind's eye. I started with that story, sketching in pencil and working to get the right facial expressions. I knew I wanted her to look a bit clueless!

All the costumes were fun for this book. I didn't try to tie them down to a specific time period or place, but I enjoyed paging through books of historical costumes, textile designs, and ancient places and dreaming up ways to use them.

Whether drawing a person, animal, or scene, everything changes as you add color. Each color you add affects your next choice. I don't completely know what something is going to look like before I start—in fact, if I knew, it wouldn't be as exciting as it is. To make a story believable, though, the characters' clothes and the settings still have to be consistent from page to page. "The Emperor's New Clothes" was especially tough because there were so many people in each of the pictures, but mostly because it's hard to figure out how to draw invisible clothes!

I'd never drawn wicked characters like the Giant, the Ogre, and the Big Bad Wolf before. It was an important challenge to get them just right since the book is for young children. I asked my family what they thought about each sketch because I didn't want them to be too scary—but I didn't want them to be wimps either!

I was concerned that people would have expectations of what a castle or the Shoemaker's home or the Gingerbread Boy would look like because these tales are such classics. I quickly found that the places and stories become your own, though. It was a surprise to feel so free to interpret and put my own spin on things. Perhaps that's another part of the timeless appeal of the stories in this collection.

I hope children discovering these tales for the first time will love them as much as I did when I was a child—and when I visited them again to create this book.